Red Town

Red Town

poems by

Judith Skillman

Silverfish Review Press

Published by Silverfish Review Press
P.O. Box 3541
Eugene, OR 97403

ISBN: 1-878851-16-0

Cover painting *Red Sun* © 1998 by Priscilla Maynard.
Cover design by Valerie Brewster, Scribe Typography.
Text design by Rodger Moody and Connie Kudura, ProtoType Graphics.

Manufactured in the United States of America.

Acknowledgments

Grateful acknowledgement is made to the editors of the following journals in which these poems first appeared, some in different versions: *Yellow Silk*, "The Woman with Fallen Breasts"; *Fine Madness*, "The Healing," "Lilacs"; *Green Mountains Review*, "*The* Accident of Water"; *Willow Springs*, "The Flaws of the World"; *Boston Literary Review*, "Recurring Violence"; *Seneca Review*, "Attic Windows"; *Arnazella's Reading List*, "Mother's Buttons"; *Mankato Poetry Journal*, "Brood Mare," "Head Injury," "Violence"; *Northwest Review*, "Bourne," "The Cutter"; *Journal of the American Medical Association*, "The Body Especial," "Parkinson's"; *Hubbub*, "A Dark Morning"; *Silverfish Review*, "The Knitting Bag," "Red Town"; *Pontoon #2*, "Colic"; *Prairie Schooner*, "Sad Breed."

I am grateful to the Centrum Foundation and to Fort Worden, where several of these poems were written.

Thanks to Jim and Karen Bodeen, Patty Cannon, Jack Gilbert, Marjorie Power, Joannie Kervran Stangeland, Carolyn Willis, John Witte, and Deborah Woodard.

Contents

"I summon the loves that, racked and followed
by summer's scythe, embalm the evening air
with their white inactivity."

–Rene Char, "Invitation"

"Childhood memories surge back more vividly midway through life—like some palimpsest whose original text suddenly reappears after the manuscript has been chemically treated."

–Gerard De Nerval, "Angélique"

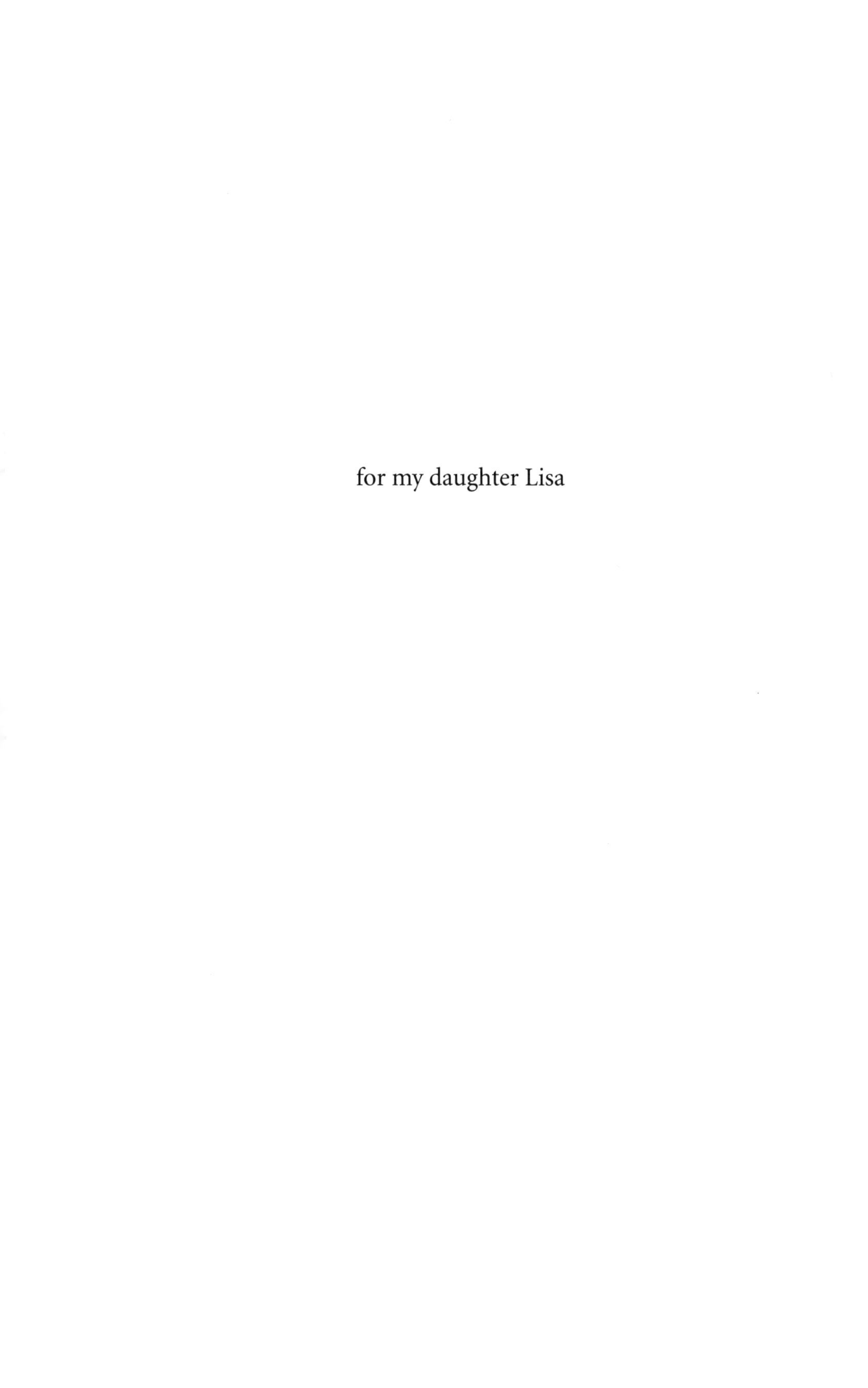

for my daughter Lisa

I. Horse Corridor

SWEET PEAS

Their fragrance dense and feminine
as the folds they bear. A bouquet of curlicues,
a mass, an overture. Today
he tugged at the earth until juniper limbs
broke free. A neighbor remarked
some folks tie them to the bumper
to break those roots: twenty-eight, almost
thirty years old. That struggle over,
they retreat to separate chambers
where he'll create autonomous systems
and she'll write short letters.
Venus followed the sun
and look what happened—
it can never rise. Setting,
it reminds her that similar bodies
remain stuck to one another.
Saturday gone forever, though it was
just three days ago. As if her better
were the sister who never calls or writes
she stands level with the flowers,
pressing her forehead toward
the center. There, if she's lucky, she'll find
the smell of hay, the horse
of sadness. Its lavender, cloven hoof
with triangular, frozen frog.

THE PLEIADES

A chipped moon rises over the snow.
A woman leans across the long table
in the lit window
and reminds her husband to take his pills.

Behind the house,
in a wooden shed, the telescope waits a long time
near the gardening tools,
with its clock drive and fancy gears.

It's stale here. There's no one left to blame.
Sleep is in the snow,
printed with a woman's boots.
A vein of black ice

is the only reminder of danger. Bluish light
presses at the windows, wanting to come in,
to make us all better. Sleep is everywhere,
waiting for permission to enter,

to lay a hand on a shoulder
and begin the business of getting well.
Inside the shed the telescope
waits to be allowed a winter full of stars.

Soon the roof will slide back.
God will see the inside of the house,
the woman prodding, the man resisting,
and through a slim crack in time

the telescope will rise and puncture the veil
of reddish-blue gasses. Planets and moons come to light,
and the sisters in partial eclipse,
the less than sane, the seven.

AFTERIMAGE

Days of living alone, sleeping alone,
taking meals at a square yellow table.
A gap in the front door, wind
pouring in, the light through slats of bamboo
too bright. Did she see God there?
Standing in her shadow, was God a germ
on the sheets or the void between weak
trails of water, when she turned on the kitchen tap
and held a plate too long, turning
its face around slowly. Cheap plastic
holding rose and turquoise flowers, designs
that would have brought a sneer in her former life.
She couldn't wait to leave His presence.
What if it wasn't God, but some offal of His, given
to her when she took her pills. She thinks
it still possible to surface
from some dream and find herself
at the foot of a strange bed under a street-lit holly tree.
God in the thick white paint of doors
whose frames have warped. In the heavy doors
that want to close, and the peeling floor
that slopes towards the straits.

CHESTNUTS

One October laid over another,
horse chestnuts swarming over the ground
in a city so unlike Paris

it would take her years to remember
why they finally sent her away.
There were vendors cluttering arterials

and at the back of a shop,
near St. Germain, she might have seen
a little smoke escaping from a window.

Like this curtain set loose and fluttering
in the hotel worker's hovel.
She glimpsed a pig turning on a spit.

One city laid over another.
Here migrant workers, there men from Nigeria
eyeing her and mouthing words.

Twenty questions. If vegetable,
an inedible fruit, lime-green and spiky.
Inside floats the doubled nut, *like testicles,* he said.

Allow this kind of timetable:
asters growing spindly,
tree tops spreading a thick luster of leaves.

Because in the end whatever's useless
and can't be made over
ends up choking the street with its brilliance.

HORSE CORRIDOR

Such dirty leaves.
They fall from the apple-pear
to blacken the ground.

The sun's fallen too,
gone from its station in the sky
to leave the earth dark
in a poor age.

In their wooden cells
horses paw the ground.
When they breathe
steam comes from their nostrils.

Scent of a girl's arm.
Lather and lather,
then they're gone, the metal combs and brushes,
soapy water
that could clean a sloppy animal.

In the southern quadrant
a gate leans into an arena.
The same trail circles the perimeter:
there she stopped and got on,

there her horse spooked
and reared.
In Lady's pen a room sways
under electric light.
I pass by, see the shovel smile,

hear the door bang shut.
Nervous starlings
pick at the ground
when I come home
these winter afternoons.

In rain-wet darkness
something grows,
but no one's certain whether
it's going to flower.

BROOD MARE

Late December under eighteen hours of lights
and she begins to come apart.

Or do I take her apart?
First her pretty red fur
peeling off in clumps.
Then the mournful eyes one at a time,
bright buttons
posing on the ground.

This is sewing.
Snip-snip.
This is the ripper
poking and unraveling
some seam or other.

So she's crazed already
when the wind begins to carry off leaves,
pieces of the pattern,
bit parts.

Just suppose hysteria works this way:
A sliver of glass finds its way in
and can't get back out.

I love her sensitive triangles,
the little frogs coated in mud.
The stony tone of detail work
that never lets go.

And God
how early in the day it is,
to be so tired.

BARN OF FATHERLESS GIRLS

The requisite stable cat wants to melt
into a pool of sunlight
cast through a Dutch door.

Stored peat exhales will o' the wisps
and a tribe of girls gathers,
tossing long manes of hair,

flashing breeches and boots.
I imagine this kind of laughter drifts
higher every summer,

until it unravels
and the shrill, unearthly sound
can be loosened by rain.

Sun streams into the yearling's stall,
and I find my daughter's *Note of Release*,
still legible, steeping in a bucket of grain.

I see the whorl
of her brushes, hear
the whisper of her long whip.

How many years
between the wildest rampage
and the shortened, watchful sleep of horses.

THE HEALING

Here is the woman who wears her hair
pinned up with chopsticks, here are
the same horses and clear troughs
holding their goldfish like foreign money.

There is the square foot of earth
under a flowering plum where the yearling
was gelded, blood
spreading into the ground
before my children.

It was a violence so deep that it went by
without apprehension. Now under thick wrapping
of shock I sleep again easily, as they do,
circling my memories of the birth,
angling diagonally across and letting it go.

Horses follow their girls.
When they pass I hear the sound of metal
shoes against dirt, that scraping
of the past. The trees wear the edge
of plum blossoms over their leather bark.

When I ask *How are your horses*
it's the same answer as before:
some are down, some up. One limps
from a sudden bolt to freedom, a run
through blackberry bushes.

There is nothing to give away the knowledge
that today is different from the other days.
The smith's hammer falls
as usual, and the strange woman
oils the reins as if winter
were a woman's name, one she gave away.

II. Lying Close to the Field

BEFOULMENT

Come night time the poppies close,
and I lose
my stranglehold on desire.
I see the buoy's intermittent light
from a kitchen
where I neglected eggs and spinach
in favor of pizza. In this way,
little by little,
what's good in us,
whatever sees into the stubborn
appetites of beauty, goes wrong.
By afternoon it seemed these flowers
were lashed and stapled by rain
to the front stoop.
How can anyone end their labor
under the pressure of the lilacs,
those heavy blossoms
bearing down? Come evening
the raccoon forages through long grass
in its organized fashion,
touching one thing and another
until it comes to the step,
where it picks up heels of bread,
its thin dark fingers
fettered by one constraint,
extremely remote,
that a half-blind animal would be born
with a thumb.

MOTHER'S BUTTONS

They are steeping in a tall jar, a jumble
of anchors and shells
ripening in mother-of-pearl light
on the cherry sill.

Like pebbles sifting toward sand
they lie about themselves.
Mother's collection of faces and pearls,
her captive audience.

They wait to trim the infant's sweater
or decorate the waistband of a skirt.
Awful marbles.
Dead eyes by handfuls wanting

to be counted, wanting to matter.
She stood with her back
to the child, facing the sink
and the window. Her hands, lost under

suds, her absent murmur,
meant she'd heard nothing
of what the child said when it talked
a blue streak.

Mother's buttons, her breasts
and ample figure, the way she took care
not to ruffle Father, seaming
complacency to fear.

I remember searching for one special signet,
hoping, among the hours,
to find a bauble. The house was bric-a-brac.
Antique light spilled through windows.

Like curios, a pile of half-price remnants
rested on the table. She sewed
one pattern piece to another, as if she could ever
turn out a whole child.

PARKINSON'S

A slowing in the nerves.
Spurred by the bony moon
and one star, an eternal nun
whose face she remembers,
she stares up at a planet
covered in mist.

The dogwood's grown so tall
she can no longer touch the flowers
that float there. At the crown
of the magnolia a few blossoms
remind her of objects
the crows could pick up and carry
if they weren't sleeping in ink.

She knows how want peels back.
Under want is numbness,
and beneath that the pity
that traps her with its color,
bright and artificial.

Huge petals float below the ceiling
of sky, its rim of cities.
Along her spine a trunk
of wood lies superimposed,
thickening with the years.

A little less dopamine left now
to cushion the urge for sex or sleep.
She wants to believe in the clear border
that might still exist
between moon and bone,
planet and star, star and flower.

PIECINGS

Like sewing needles
falling sharply
a fine rain anchors the house
to its landscape of ornamental pear,
lodge pole pine, and strafed grass...
Stitch-stitch. I tongue
thread. Thread enters
the eye of the needle,

drizzle whets
the ground of a place I keep separate.
Home.
No, I don't need needles.
Give me a diaper, a flannel cloth,
a kerchief to wipe dust
from teardrop leaves of weeping fig.

It falls all day long, rain not wet enough
to coax a Japanese maple
back from oblivion.

Remember Win's needles? So dull
she didn't use a thimble. Only bag balm
for the pads of her fingers.

This rain's not clean enough to strip
grit from the sky
or bring back Crimson Glory.
Fifteen years ago, after my second labor,
my husband, awkward in the ward, proffered a flower.
Drizzle covers sounds, masks
the clash of tribes and causes, crows and Quakers.
There was a gray logic I kept inside,
a horror of filth and words.
I kept the rain stripes there, hidden
after a series of days as dark as night.

DYSPHORIA

Once the clock was famous,
there was a state of health in the nation.

Coffee perked,
the kettle sat under its crocheted cover.

Don’t be mum. Don’t slouch so
in and out of depression.

Remember there was singing sometimes.
She who had many faces has been reduced to one.

A tourist in a small town outside Paris,
she lay with her head in the grass

and watched the horses pick their way.
The American man in tall black boots

stood with a long whip, saying
Look where you’re going and go where you’re looking.

FROST-CLOTH

Indecent starts pose
at the bare-bones beginning,
as if Spring
could think itself into being.

The crocus unfurls
like a green flag
willing to be nipped in the bud.

Why so early? Why the intimation
of a place to sleep
under the open sky,
under dead stars sprinkled like salt?

What wants to bloom,
wafting across an open field
searched so many times
it's only memory?

Someone come with a painter's drop cloth,
a yard of flannel, a sheet
taken from beneath a man and a woman
making love.

What begins can be blunted,
blighted. Revolution starts
as a matrix of blossoms
brown-nosing the air.

Someone come and cover them up,
before they inherit the earth.

FLAWS OF THE WORLD

These are the smaller flaws,
    how much dirt covers canvas,
    how big the fissure
of recurrent illness a child must cross

in order to be well again.
    Bellini's smiling lady emerges
    once more from her dark collar
of oil. She will happen

beneath the paint of landscapes forgers
    imagine, her headdress still blazing
    like a lily next to a torrent.
She will be unveiled in cures

the virus surrounds with its permeable borders
    of water, and she exists as a flower
    not smothered by badly-done huts,
not taken in by any version that occurs

to the false artists. They sit in halls
    on hard chairs, adding more detail
    to a hat than a necklace, putting
their own ideas into the acquittals

of light. A surface can be made white
    again, doused in gesso.
    Still the rose, wired and staked
to its homemade frame, is overtaken by blight

in its third year, while alyssum
    scrawls wide messages in dirt,
    broad signatures of scent, headier
than the woman who stayed behind to disarm

DaVinci. He is seated with a knife
    before a blank canvas.
    Before we can begin, we must
learn to see our male and female sides,

that pool flowering across the world,
    the smoke that turns spindles
    to towers. The hills are powder,
the Nicene horses have been bred,

and everything depends upon such
    rituals as a small child might invent,
    one beaten for its game: holding onto a smile,
already beginning to know too much.

THE WOMAN WITH FALLEN BREASTS

Sits in an acrylic spa,
confesses to me
while we talk around
issues. Outside
a few dogwoods
have been deceived
into flower.

The woman with fallen breasts
sits closer to me
than I have ever been
to a woman. There is water
falling with the melody
peculiar to water.
There are soaps
in the shapes of turtles
and roses, and little strings
that curl on the blade
of the scissors.

Everything has gone well,
I say, has transpired
according to plan.
We are sitting
on wooden slats
and her hands
aren't clasped over her head,
so there is nothing
to lift them up by,
the hollow forms
on their brown circles
and stems, stretch lines
crossing and recrossing,
saying in their fine hand

We have given away
the blue cloud lying
close to the field,
we have kept nothing.

III. Dark Mornings

BOURNE

When the Cherry
rustles above her head
she hardly realizes
why she leaves
her clothes on the rocks,

passes a hand absently
through water
as if smoothing
an infant's forehead.
Instead she takes the fruit

pressed into her hand
and watches the bloody stone
wet her fingers.
Wasn't sweetness always
a symbol for their falling.

She walks with the man
along the river bank
until they come to know
the sore places
in the soles of their feet,

the fish knifing away.
Under the currents
every death moves in time
towards them,
each cliché is soothed

into language
as if there were
no way to limit
Paradise, other than
this that has already happened.

DELICATESSEN

Layers of cold meat
pinked at the edges,
a ruffle of lettuce,
and the hard bun shut like a lid.

The store finally dark,
heat leaving through windows,
the tiny exhausted vacuum inside
each electric light bursts.

The countless others
who came and went
all gone, their languages
joined to others

by a single root
hoarded from the Old Country.
Rye and poppy seeds
skitter across the floor,

an army of doughy women
turns broad backs
and ample breasts away from me.
They take back their laps

where I sat
like an offering
and had my cheeks pinched
to see if they were done.

RED TOWN

Maybe where I live.
The prostitute posing in a window
in Amsterdam,
that evening when I walked with my uncle.
He wanted to show her to me.
Not coal dark.
There is a woman in a red dress
and black laced boots
who sits on a metal chair
above ground.
The starch is dry.
This miner's wife, stranded on the earth.

THE CUTTER

Behind my back he stands,
wearing his skull cap
in Talmudic darkness.
The patterns laid out
on long tables, suit coats
and trousers poised
to be born. Garment maker,
cutter, would be engineer—
the blank days of the calendar
fill with arms and legs
that rise from the table
with their needs intact,
like the dead.
He thinks all this
hard work ought to earn him
safety, keep the fingers pointing
straight. What's a ghetto
but a place to put in
a sixteen-hour day, a land
of shapes skewered from nothing.
The trees keep their tweed,
and the plants have forward
motion to propel them
into flower, but he keeps
coming into the shop,
adjusting his pins
under a bare bulb
tied to a string.
The halves of his life,
quartered, come into my own,
and I turn to my cousin,
saying how beautiful it is
to live in the service

of Venus, and we wonder
what the four years
meant to him, all those
fancy men and women
stylish in the face of his dullness,
the scissors eking it out,
the blunt sun rising
in a sky sewn shut.

THE KNITTING BAG

House of the circular needle, and the hooks.
From its open mouth a thread oozed
into her lap, and up over her shoulder
like another sister.

A tapestry where the deep forest
refracts and birds are quiet.
They never said we were Irish twins.
I take the bottle back after she is born.

Each strand twisted and slivered,
the same lie coming from one mouth
in meditation, in boredom, in the car
with its glassy fears.

A handle shaped like a stirrup,
a hot shoe. Finicky eaters,
we steal off to eat chocolate,
to rub our hands on red carpeted stairs.

A hovel, a pigsty, a lackluster confidante,
when did our mother's face go to stubble?
How long will I keep her here
in exile, in the bag

with its twisted remnants
the long and short intestine, length
of a football field. There is a heart-shaped
uterus with a septum,

there are missing teeth and kidneys,
like products, continually emerging
from the woodsy bag. Now she is
a grandmother in earnest.

The delicate dreams are complications.
I hear them talking in other languages
in half tones, in that room held apart
by its makeshift divider.

A DARK MORNING

My eyes burn from too little sleep.
There are strangers in the house.
I can hear them
talking downstairs, their laughter growling
like hunger.

The sun must be eclipsed.
My sister caused this to happen,
I think, by staring at a brown spider. Once
she saw the moon and the sun
in the sky together
and christened a basement room with her panic.

Father collected still shots
of her disease, checking
the progress of straw axes and hills,
taking special care to preserve
the craters that form a necklace
from a cold rim—Bailey's beads.

I know, like memory,
that the sun spends its own image
in coins across the ground. A wet nurse
likes to siphon the same flagging crescent
through each leaf
of background foliage.

My sister and I thrived for thirteen years
on surprise: the sun halved
by a pinhole, the sun brazen as a slip
in a cardboard box,
the saving grace of paper plates.

If I rinse my face
and walk downstairs,
an ancient table will be set
with black-eyed Susans,
centers the color of rosin.

RECURRING VIOLENCE

At first it's the isolation
of the child who needs you,

of Ornamental Plums
fused over streets.

In the fragrance something comes to you—
a note, a thought you dismiss

as a character who claims no relation.
Now there are two of you,

the easy woman who ministers
to the others,

and her pale sister sweating glass.
You shake the house inside out,

notice dents and holes
made by a leg of furniture

or a fist. You name the children
a second time, get rid of the ethnic

undertones. In this picture you have grown
large, pregnant with forgetting.

COLIC

I can still hear the crying,
the harsh swell of tones
close to evening when other houses
stop bustling and fall silent.
The one who won't sleep—
I hear her. Her thumb curls
like a shell frozen in a stone,
and the exchange begins,
cell walls broken and flooded
by the sea, trees losing
their resiliency beneath the oceans—
how their crowns wave.
It's a trellis I braid. Someone's
gone soft on account of money.
Someone's lost their life savings
playing Russian roulette.
No one cares if a child cries.
The wheel turns, the freeways close in,
the cows low and turn their huge ugly
faces down to earth but no one
comes to comfort them.
When they cut the injured horse open
they'll find infection and we
will be the worse for having heard.

TO ONE WHO IS INTIMATE WITH SICKNESS

Its secret paths and weather,
phlegm's and fevers.

Its bowls and straws,
white sheets and nightmares.

Its cold baths and glaring bulbs,
little words that mean nothing.

To the nurse of dead children
huddled with sore throats

returned from their delirium
centuries later by penicillin.

Give me a single reason why the sick
should be trusted on their cots in the dark.

A pillow is a ration of bread
belonging to a special friend,

a pillow is a wooden chest
hoarding its hunk of bread.

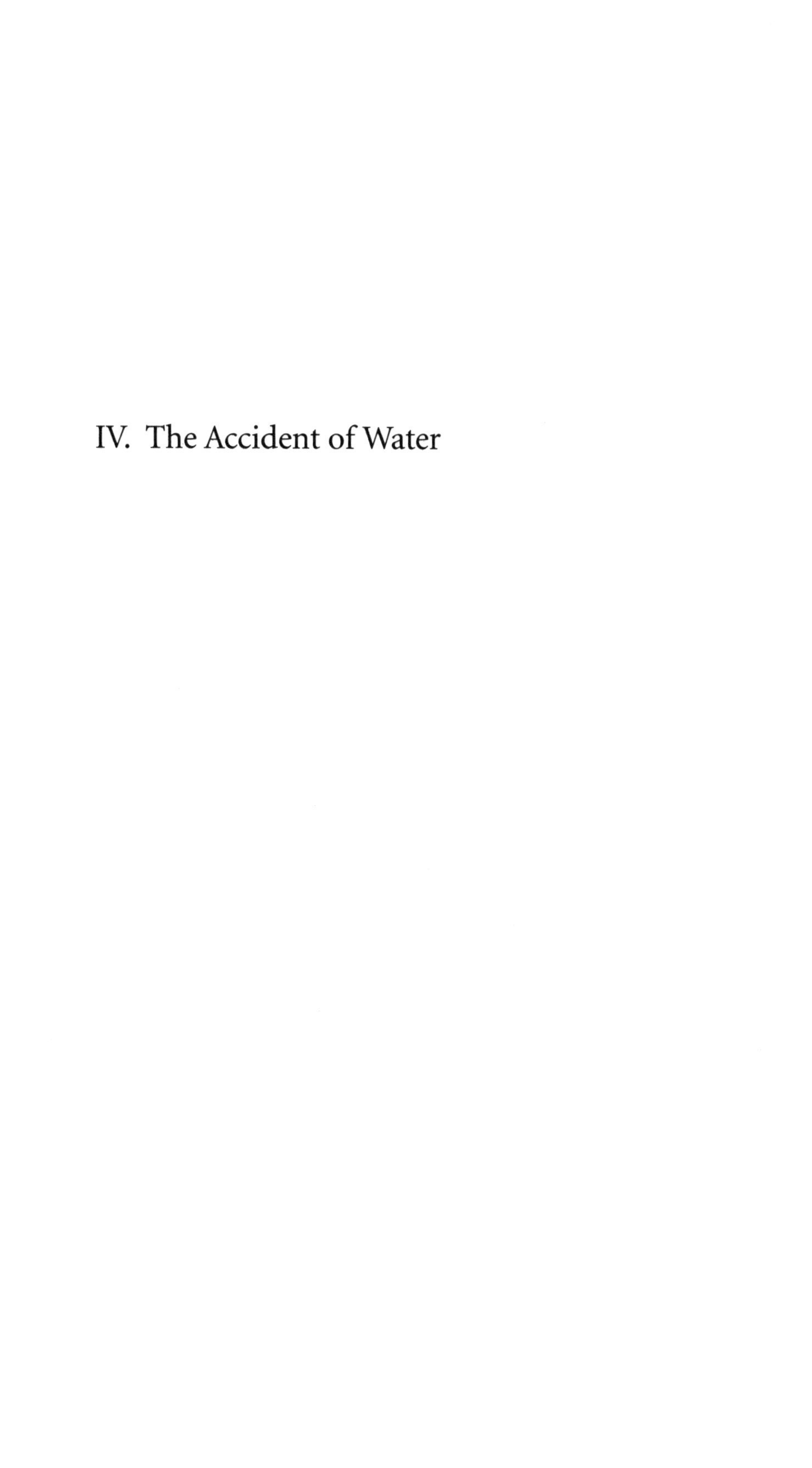

IV. The Accident of Water

THE YVETTE

I had a dream of danger:
Camus' woman drowning in the Seine
a second time
and a third.

I was bound by a long brown cord
to a town called "Bures."
The bubbles in my mouth
surprised me.

How narrow we were in those days,
walking rows of stone steps
to the boucherie. Inside the rabbits
lined up, spooning

with their cold flesh
and furless bodies
bequeathed to death,
little paws arranged just so.

The glass eyes were always open
to see all that must have happened
in those early days
of adolescence.

A woman can exist
on a pedestal but a river
empties its brown waters
daily, ensconced in a town of scientists.

LILACS

Because they signify a life
less sterile, I twist their stems
like the woman in Eliot's *Portrait.*

Only the ones which fall and catch on long grass
can be brought into the house,
which is small and cheap and faces the sea.

A strong dose of fatigue where once was longing.
I twist lilac stems and wait for the grosbeak
to come to the fork of the tree.

Dried flowers dangle near the ornament,
an umbrella for hanging pots on.
Invented by the French, I'm sure.

I twist their stems. They brown now,
May turning into June,
the beach sterile. When I walk there

I pick up pebbles and drop them back down
to hear the sound of stone on sand.
A mussel glows blue but the lilac's

tawdry blooming merely means
one kind of fatigue has passed away
to be replaced by another.

In my mouth the taste of rice vinegar.
I lean towards the crooked trunk whittled clean
and catch the scent of another aesthetic.

Compliments behoove the lady in me
to find a small start of green
somewhere in the garden.

Anything alive can be felt between the fingers.
The crows line their nests
with these kinds of straws.

THE ACCIDENT OF WATER

The woman with scissors
still wakens at night,
thinks she hears
the unmistakable pop of pipes

followed by the sound of a shower
drenching a grieving woman.
A premise of normalcy ruptured
and she woke up soaked

in sweat, faced with Noah's flood,
ship-wrecked
by her own house.
She heard water pouring

from the water heater,
dragging its liquid fingers
across a tile floor, water
biting off the tops of flowers,

molding stems
and wrenching babies
from between their mother's legs.
Now wherever the good life

dares to lay its head
torrents of water
go on dragging the cliff down,
its scalloped face.

A cable snaps
and the gondola
that could take her out of here
rusts to memory.

The second accident
is the one
that waits to happen
once she's woken to the first.

CHILD DAYS

On the first day
an acrid square of field
grew swollen,
sewed to another
by a rille of water.

A nest bloomed in a tree
and I said, *this part is and this isn't.*
Winter can't prevent
what's hidden
from coming out.

There were sticks floating
into the mouth of the garage,
gutters full of leaves and filth.
I was going farther in
toward the birthplace of Jake

and birthplace of Aaron,
a length of coastline
swaying in the wind.
Even for the flag of no country
stitching accrues.

Birthplace of Sarah, and Ida,
the aunts swallowed whole
by uncles, swept under
like the Three Graces
with their smiles intact.

*

Bottomed out.
Under the sleight of words

and the kiss of origins,
inside that cyst where fluid
mimics blood.

Within the nest, wanting
to float off unaware,
nomadic, to wander
under the weight of infinitives
until, restored by the power

of blank days
the other places and persons
came back to me.
A field in which a needle,
gap-toothed, looked for its thimble.

The thimble a tumbrel of weeds
and an old woman
carrying a chicken
to the wise man,
who would say

if the blood ran clean.
The separation
of milk and meat,
the thin bread, and balls
that rose or sank like fishes.

*

Grease skimmed the surface of broth
where chicken eggs
floated, iridescent. We had organ
meat, scanty rations, tenement
houses open to the wind

that leaned in
as for Shiva.
This neighbor never left,
that one was taken,
that one arrived to sicken.

In pockets
the cutlery lies, a slave.
The nest settles
at the crotch of the tree.
Order predominates in stars and cycles.

The moon is new,
greater, lesser, swollen full.
Like women it fills
and empties and lathers
the skies.

*

The field's a square of chocolate,
impinged on in sweetness
and filth until the tooth
aches to be taken
from its hole.

The cyst's an abscess
that waits to be cleaned by a needle.
In it hair, orange-blood,
and fluid coalesce
to the point of lucidity.

The aunts are different.
They wait for the other shoe
to drop, they walk on eggs,
they season meat,
yield, entreat.

CRIMSON GLORY

A sluggish aphid
steps from petal
to petal, sucking juice
that will fatten the hours
and call the children
in to dinner. Their games
go on, hollow words
that rhyme,
metered questions
rising and falling on wind
singed by smoke from a car fire.

Now the heavy blossom
lifts an iota, now it plunges
further towards ruin,
but always it is her face,
hair hidden by a kerchief,
gypsy eyes darkening
as they behold an earth
that crawls with creatures
each one smaller than the next,
all bent on carrying crumbs
from here to there,
soldiering the body
of a fellow with bent arms
and missing legs.

How can she bear it,
I wonder, watching
the blunt petals open
again to perfume the air,
tasting her scent
on my wrists and shoulders,
watching the curve of her back
that never breaks
under the strain of blooming.

BARGAINING

for Patty Cannon

The full moon through French panes—
bright as chalk. In the fragments
something brightens,
the mind of God fastened to natural designs.

A web glows,
benign spider like a woman's life at the center:
mathematical plans and an inclination
for romance that can't be satisfied.

The moon from behind a trailing branch
of fir assaults her with its sisterly light.
She can't help staring though she knows
how moonlight attaches

to her thoughts, keeps her up nights.
It's like that with the cycles of the body,
as if the spider were Buddha,
its fat belly swaying above this street

that follows the same arc
up and back, and she not learning
anything anymore, unless it is to pay
for a fit of conscience with wakefulness,

to exchange a day of sickness
for an hour of clarity.

THE BODY ESPECIAL

I said I had almost forgotten about the sick.
Their glazed eyes, their little fevers are spawning
the same conclusions. We go in, and the day
yawns open, white pieces of sky pinned back.

A room. It always begins in a space
with a narrow table. Here are the eminent
details—the useless magazines,
acres of acoustic ceiling, and squares
of gauze that wait for tongs and silence.

But it wasn't there, exactly. Although
it began there, and took on the slight heartbeat
of arrhythmia, due, we speculated,
to a gratuitous electric shock.
I remember leaping backwards.
Epiphany took me by the shoulders,
no less.

I say it began there. And changed, overnight,
to black pockets of fluid, caught up, dire,
needy—those places in the second body
I carried.

*

El Nino comes again with its red spot, a bruise,
a septicemia clinging to the coast,
bringing this rabid girl with it. Her hair
is tangled, so I lean in close, thinking
I'll study the overlapping strands, and finally
decipher the rat's nests.

The child throws pills at me and wanders off
into a dream. A version of herself,
ripe with cysts and strong urine.
Samples leak from odd containers

until she spawns a sister
who grows an anomaly when her ovaries
kick in—*size of a mandarin orange,*
we were lucky: these words
spoken underwater, by a surgeon
in green.

PASTORAL

Aphrodite, Narcissus, and Echo—still dreamy from long walks
in the woods, closeted together
in a cabin near the water.

The beautiful one wants to know the one who doesn't speak
for fear of repeating herself. So she removes one wall
and makes a stage of the living room.

The one who loves himself wants to know more about the water,
its wavelets and the silt carried off by foam to rebuild a coastline.
He questions a lighthouse taken away from ships.

He positions himself next to the dripping faucet.
The women touch one another's skin,
marbled like madronas.

Strange that the beautiful one would love someone
of her own kind, that the one who speaks in echoes
would refuse to dabble in the theater.

Finished with each other, the women preen, fluff their hair,
rouge. The man can stare only forward or down
so they position themselves in front and below.

In the sink there's not enough water for him to drown,
so he turns to another form
of self-aggrandizement: flexing his biceps.

But his trunk's grown too thick
to bend, and the room is a painter's studio
furnished with curtains, mirrors, and artificial fruits.

The two women become more beautiful and repetitious.
The man pulls another man from thin air
and pins this twin to a dais.

V. The Word *Blood*

PAPERWHITES

We could be brother and sister.
In the incestuous, blue light of winter,
our lives play out in a paperweight.
There's a kitchen
at the back of the house—
its red roof and tiny porch.

The snow is another matter.
Lightweight flakes rise and fall.
Nothing to pin down
in a vacuum.
I would like to write letters to you,
scented missives,
white sheets pleated with secrets.

THE WORD *BLOOD*

Each time we raise our glasses
the word *blood* gets said.
This time is like the others—
no one knows why the man
his name was Elmo
with no front teeth will be remembered
for thirty years, carried forward
into the future to be spit out
at dinner. *A busboy*
at the country club
he ate from their plates
when no one was looking.
Three generations
sit together and no one believes
what comes from the lips
of a thick crystal vase
given to us by the dead.
Striped tulips opening while we talk.

SAD BREED

My father meant to be kind when he cussed.
His cussing couldn't be helped.
The consonants had to come out,
at breakfast, lunch, and dinner, especially
when Mother served his favorite meals, pot roast
or veal stew simmered slowly
all afternoon over the gas burner.

I don't mean to be unkind to my father
by calling attention to his disease.
Kindness is a difficult thing to measure.
It could be that helpfulness
is out of order. The wind knocks
but doesn't enter, knowing
we are better off without its testy breath
in our houses.

The wild rose
scratches at our walls as if it wants to come in,
but it would bloody our sheets.
Shoes are full of odors,
and windows rattle,
but there was never a man as kind
as my father, who said *shit.*
That word *shit* he held onto like a lifeboat
in bad weather. A hatless fellow,
a short Jewish man, hissing.

VIOLENCE

The stars cold, dry, and hard.
Thistles at the road's edge
and leaves larger than hands,
each one fallen with the same sound,
the thin crackle of applause.

How in sickness we're made again.
How we go on sadly, apart.
With breath and wetness, the scrabbling
of creatures against tree bark.
Of the mind's wandering

in and out of lucidity, the burn
of sex. And afterwards, to take
the argument one step further,
towards its penultimate conclusion:
the body. Away from the blank eyes

and the stench that means
we have risen into each other.

HEAD INJURY

Now as then the cripples
rise in the forest, where birds by the hundreds
bathe and the sun pours in by accident.
Not to know how or why
memory occurs, or what was prefigured:
the not-to-know grows daily
in the forest, where moss sinks its teeth in
and the selvages become lined, avenues
of leaves. So much gorgeous red
goes on showing itself
a by-product, place-holder, ruffle
of the diligent shadow that keeps
these things under wraps. Even for cripples
there is a listing, a sadness, and dreams
of danger, being pursued by the others.
Of the events themselves, say only
that we were present. We saw or felt or heard
the *yesses* in tiny letters and numbers
etched in bark and knot holes,
and *no*, we said, and again *no*.

SPORE

During the night heavy rains.
A spate of chills,
then the worrying,
the child who couldn't sleep
ground down to hysteria
beside a narrow bed.

The closet with its slats,
its long dresses
and unworn blouses,
only a coffin-width between her and me,
this boundary
padded with clothing.

And now I remember
she was always hyper vigilant.
Even when they carried her
on their shoulders
or bought her a fresh bed,
the northern train spelled out her name
in staccato, told her
she would never be picked up and carried along
like a log or a feather.

JUPITER

Even though none of the old charms
work anymore, I can still walk out
under this swollen star
rooted in the sky over suburbia.
It takes its place in a landscape
swept of constellations.
Now that there are no more
stories, and no reason
for the sadness, the pills, or the quarrels,
it shivers, and its metallic light
travels a long way
to bring me news.
The tallest firs have been decapitated,
cut into logs and sold.
If a body lies buried
between the pruned skyline
and the heavens full of talk,
no one needs to know.
If I turn away from the stars
I used to name, drain elixir
from a glass, if sugar burns
to a crust on the stove
while I stand in the yard cursing,
if they call me a *Wiccan*
because I refuse to swallow any more science,
still this star will shine until it sets
in a dry pocket beside the earth
and lies hidden with the others.

THE HAND BESIDE THE ROAD

There it lies, disconnected from the body,
a pink glove waving politely
in deference to its own dismemberment.
As though there were other instruments

it could have played: forceps, cello, steering wheel,
it lies there contained by handedness,
its oddness a frontier the driver remarks on
before continuing forward in the dark.

The quintessential hand
delivered from its body,
no longer asking for anything other
than an informed discussion of its origins.

Was the hand an artifact?
Did it come directly to man from God,
when His hands, still yucky from creation,
yielded their manifold copies?

Was the hand a conformist by nature?
Was its greed obvious to the objects it reached for?
When did it manage to encircle them? How did it plan
for death, other than grasping at straws?

What about poetry, music, art? Was the medium
meant to be its only joy? Tearing at wood, stone, notes,
and flesh with the same impartial strokes,
using the thumb to finger and count.

Because the sinister origin of the hand is a subject
whose implications may be grasped
only by the chance:
a second hand lying close by, in the median strip.

ATTIC WINDOWS

The shelf of a dark perspective
has deepened, but there is no deception
in the simple fabric, or in the birds beyond.
Their pleated wings are dovetailed
like fry, or fingerlings. Evening sun
lights the water.

Call such a place Spring,
where every crumb of leavened bread
clings to its corner
until it can be discovered by a feather,
brought to bear.

As the ledge of the window
gives credence to the view beyond,
the cut frame relinquishes
its shallow claim on me
and the needle pumps,

a stripe of light piercing these fields
in the midst of plenty,
pinning a strange bird to its tree.
In the mind of the quilt maker,
flowers and stars have already
begun to state their similarities.

By the time we have noticed
the bird, whether or not it belongs to the landscape
is academic, a theory
that thrives on the abundance
of certain patterns repeated by the blood.

Call this farmland, the area
between borders and ancestors.
They link supine hands
in twos and threes, and their symbols,
shank bone and salt,
are indelible marks made by a woman.

She sits in her catholic chair,
evenings, holding their history
in her lap, finishing up
the flowers, hearts, and stars.

if it wanted to. And later, the triangular scar
on its porcelain cheek would be a point
of interest.

But no one can have the dolls' wad
of material, folded and unfolded,
passed around dense shoulders like a sari,
until intrigue, and a child's slim delight